for Albie

Contents

HUBERT HORATIO

How to Raise your Grown-ups

First published
in Great Britain
by
HarperCollins *Children's Books* in 2018
HarperCollins *Children's Books* is a division of HarperCollins*Publishers* Ltd,
HarperCollins Publishers
1 London Bridge Street
London SE1 9GF

The HarperCollins website address is
www.harpercollins.co.uk

1

ISBN 978–0–00–826408–6

Lauren Child asserts the moral right to be identified
as the author and illustrator of the work.

Original text design by David Mackintosh
Printed and bound in England by CPI Group (UK) Ltd, Croydon CR0 4YY

LAUREN CHILD

HUBERT HORATIO

How to Raise your Grown-ups

HarperCollins Children's Books

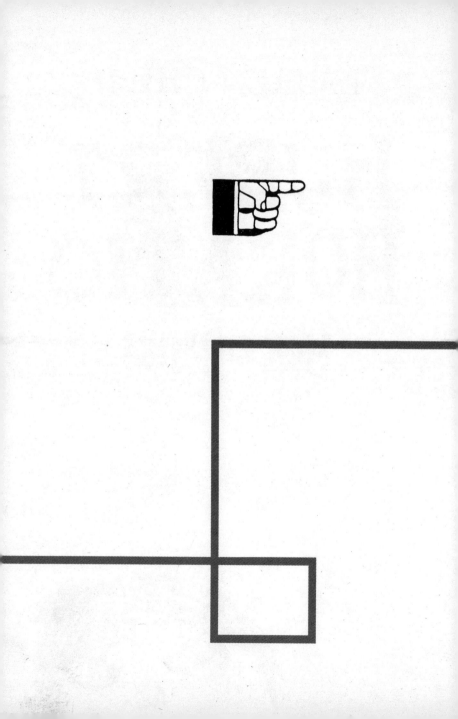

PREFACE

THESE STORIES ARE ALL SET IN THE PAST —
in those *carefree* years long before the Bobton-
Trent family had fallen on hard financial times.
Before they'd had to sell off all their most valuable
possessions and so leave their mansion, Sweeping
Acres, for pastures new — otherwise known as
number 17b Plankton Heights.

These stories are about the days when the
Bobton-Trents had it cushy, very cushy indeed.

Yes, those days were the days.

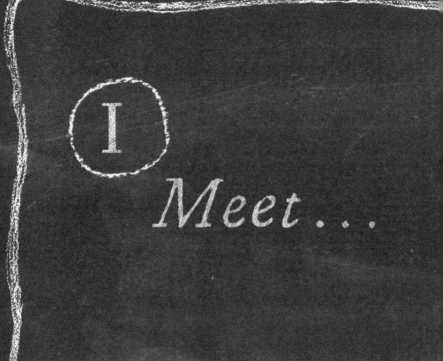

I

Meet...

the

Bobton-

Trents

MR AND MRS BOBTON-TRENT

LOVED PEOPLE

THEY LOVED EATING IN RESTAURANTS AND conversing with the diners who happened to be sitting at adjacent tables. They loved the daily chats with Mr and Mr Lyle – their neighbours to the east. They loved bumping into friends in the park. They loved bumping into strangers in the street. They delighted in chance encounters with interesting artists and friendly builders. They enjoyed waving hello to newspaper boys and newspaper girls and shouting good morning to the police, the traffic wardens and whoever might be waiting for the lights to change at a pedestrian crossing. They were happy when talking with the woman who came to clean the pool filter and they were happy when laughing with the man who came to shampoo the carpets. They adored meeting anyone and everyone, but the person they adored the most was their one and only child . . .

HUBERT HORATIO
BARTLE BOBTON-TRENT

(or HUBERT HORATIO for short
or HUBERT for very short *or sometimes just H)*.

"He's INCREDIBLE!"

"He's got such small toes."

"When do you think he'll be able to play
TWISTER?"

They loved him so much that they never
thought to have any more children. It was
impossible to imagine that they could like
anyone as much as they liked Hubert. And he
was remarkable. An interesting child: peculiarly
mature for his age, keen to have a go at *everything*
and delighted to talk to *anyone*.

AND he was clever.

Very, very clever.

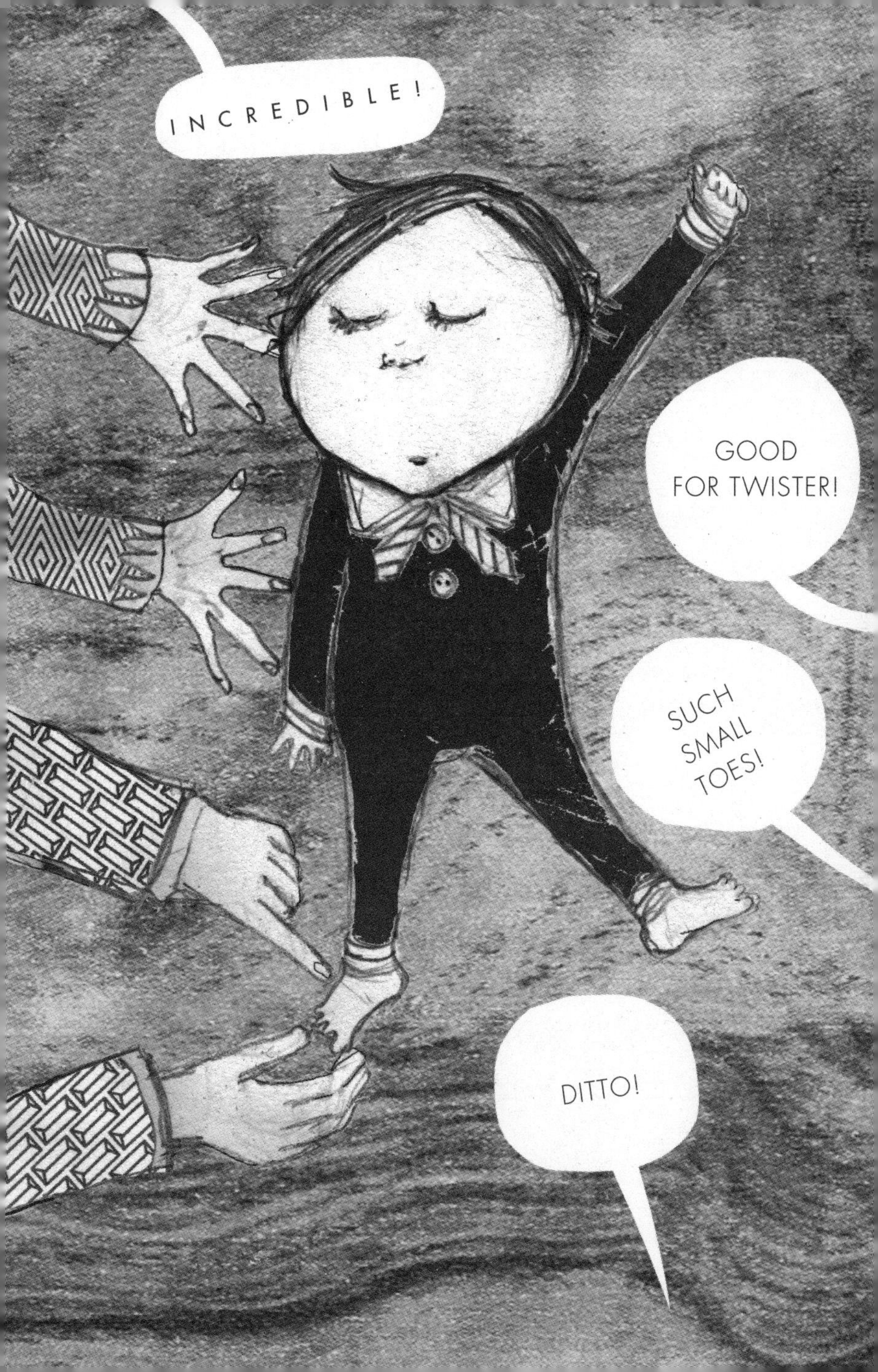
INCREDIBLE!
GOOD FOR TWISTER!
SUCH SMALL TOES!
DITTO!

i.

A Talented Child

☛ *Hubert is seen wearing
the Darblet Cap of Honour
(size 6¾).*

HUBERT
A TALENTED CHILD

HUBERT HORATIO BARTLE BOBTON-TRENT WAS, in fact, a child genius – probably the cleverest boy you will ever meet – and he could do a great many things very well.

I won't list them all here because it is an extremely long list, and lists are generally boring to read, though I will mention three of his many triumphs:

THE PRiZes ANd THE PLAUDiTS

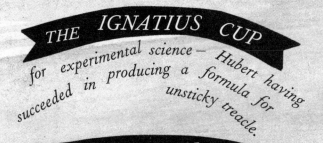

THE IGNATIUS CUP
for experimental science — Hubert having
succeeded in producing a formula for
unsticky treacle.

THE GRANTHORN PLATTER
for spelling extremely long words,
understanding their meanings and derivations,
and perfectly applying them to a sentence.

THE PLIMPTON BOWL
for ambidextrous handwriting.

[HUBERT HAD BEEN TAUGHT CALLIGRAPHY
*by Ed Felt, a cousin of his mother's and a leading
expert in the field of very good handwriting.*]

The art of gastromancy* depends upon the emission of
an audible borborygmus** from the subject.

[*Gastromancy — NOUN
A form of divination by interpreting
sounds coming from the stomach.
From the Ancient Greek, *gaster*
(the belly) + *manteia* (divination).]

[**Borborygmus — NOUN
A rumbling or gurgling sound
in the stomach.
From the Greek *borborygmós*
(intestinal rumbling).]

Those who engage in floccinaucinihilipilification*
may not appreciate the pleasure to be found in a
sesquipedalian** use of language.

[**Sesquipedalian — ADJECTIVE
Tending to use very long words.
From the Latin *sesqui* (one and a half)
+ *ped* (a foot).]

[*Floccinaucinihilipilification — NOUN
The action or habit of estimating something as worthless.
From the Latin *flocci, nauci, nihili, pili*
(words meaning "at little value") + *fication*.]

❧ *THE ARTS* ...

Hubert was an excellent painter and was

accomplished in both the Renaissance tradition . . .

Title: Fifth Avenue Traffic Roar

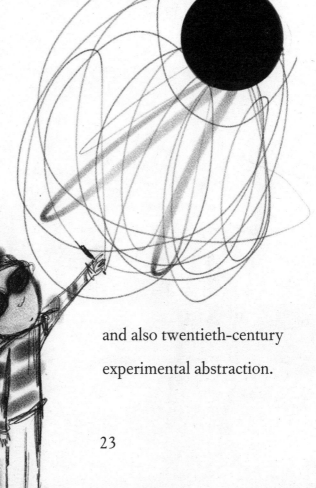

and also twentieth-century

experimental abstraction.

23

By the age of four, his work – often confused with that of the Spanish artist Pablo Picasso (1881–1973) – regularly appeared in many famous international galleries.

24

His
sculpture
was also
beginning
to show
promise.

A year after taking up contemporary dance choreography . . .

Hubert's "Elastic Formations in Shadow: No. 25" . . .

had been performed across Europe.

THERE WASN'T MUCH HUBERT *DIDN'T* EXCEL AT,

but *haiku*,

flower-arranging

and

cake-baking

were, for some

INEXPLICABLE reason,

subjects he just could NOT master.

Hubert Horatio Bartle Bobton-Trent was not a giver-upper and could often be found

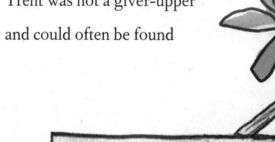

in the Japanese garden composing verse,

in the conservatory intertwining stems

or in the kitchen practising the art

of patisserie . . .

though regrettably he
never improved.

Perhaps it was his deep frustration at his
inability to succeed at these three beloved pursuits
(no matter how he struggled) which caused
Hubert to suffer on occasion from insomnia.*

[*Insomnia – NOUN: Being unable to sleep.
From the Latin *insomnis*, (sleepless), from *in-*
(expressing negation) + *somnus* (sleep).]

He battled this NOT by counting sheep
but by reciting pi.

3.141592653589793

Hubert could recite pi not only while wide awake but also in his sleep.

[FOR THOSE OF YOU WHO DON'T KNOW *(which by the way is perfectly understandable) pi is the ratio of the circumference of a circle to its diameter . . . Clear? No? Never mind — think of it as a very long number — in fact, a never-ending one. For this reason Hubert always woke up before he had made it all the way through to the end.*]

Hubert had a remarkable command of
numbers. He was very good at counting.
He kept a weather eye on the footsie[100]*,
the Dow** and the NASDAQ*** but preferred to
invest his money in local inventors, entrepreneurs
and artists, such as Mr Perry and his troupe of
dancing mice. Hubert saved all the money he made
and put it along with his pocket money into his
Spanish china pig, for he had set his heart on

SOMETHING special.

[* *The footsie – actually FTSE, which stands for Financial Times Stock Exchange.*]

[** *The Dow Jones – a daily measurement of stock exchange prices.*]

[*** *The NASDAQ – National Association of Securities Dealers Automated Quotations System – a digital system for stock trading.*]

 ii.

Millionaires

ABOUT THE BOBTON-TRENTS MONEY

YOU SEE, THE BOBTON-TRENTS WERE WHAT ARE known as *millionaires*. They had houses here and penthouses there, and exotic pets roamed the gardens. Gardens that were dotted with lakes and ponds and fountains and swimming pools. Swimming pools that were kidney-shaped and

swimming pools that were the shape of Italy

and swimming pools that were the *size* of Italy –

that's an exaggeration by the way but you surely

get my point: they had a lot of land.

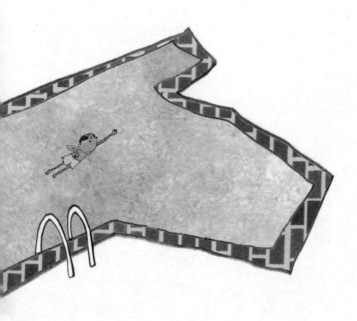

They owned islands and forests and mountains, as well as many other much SMALLER things like rare pompom mice and tiny cars big enough only for rare pompom mice to drive.

THEY WEREN'T JUST RICH – THEY WERE *EXTRAVAGANTLY* RICH!

SO rich that Mrs Bobton-Trent often found that she didn't have enough diamond-encrusted jewellery boxes to house her diamond-encrusted brooches.

And Mr Bobton-Trent would not think twice about spreading caviar (a topping a lot of people consider a bit of a treat) on his morning slice of warm toast.

They had *never* considered how much money they had in the bank because they had *never* needed to know – you see, the money *never* seemed to run out. Perhaps it was for this reason that Mr Hamburg, the bank manager, always sent them a personally signed company Christmas card and, on occasion, a voucher to spend at the local newsagent owned by his brother.

[INCIDENTALLY, *Beluga caviar must be spread using a non-metal utensil so as not to taint the flavour of that most expensive fish roe.*]

Christmas Wishes

So what did they do with all their money?

ANSWER: *everything!*

They dined out, they joined clubs, they travelled the world, they met people, they visited people, they saw things, they bought things, they built things, they donated things, they took classes in things, they learned things, they played things, but most of all . . .

they ENTERTAINED!

[The Bobton-Trents knew a great many people.]

Why... these are the best crudités I've ever tasted!

There's nothing Mrs B-T can't do with a vegetable, that's for sure.

Hubert's backhand is superb!

Nearly as good as his forehand!

"Helloo. How do you do?"

THEY VERY MUCH ENJOYED Socialising and Making Friends. Mr and Mrs Bobton-Trent were never happier than when conversing with a stranger or adding a new name to their address book.

They knew everyone, well, almost
everyone, and anyone they didn't know
they made a point of getting to know.

"People are *so* interesting" was something
Mr and Mrs Bobton-Trent were very fond of
saying. And they *did* know some *very* interesting
people.

Take, for example, close family friend
Professor Litchen. She's the one who invented
that most useful of household items, the Soap Soap
(basically soap for cleaning soap).*

And there was Mr Edgar Grimpton who lived
in a tree on Lambton Street. No one quite knew
why or how he had come to make his house in a

"Franklin Bobton-Trent, delighted to meet you."

tree but he was happy and, as Mr Bobton-Trent so often remarked, "So long as a person is happy, that's all right with me."

The Bobton-Trents usually took tea with Mr Grimpton fortnightly.

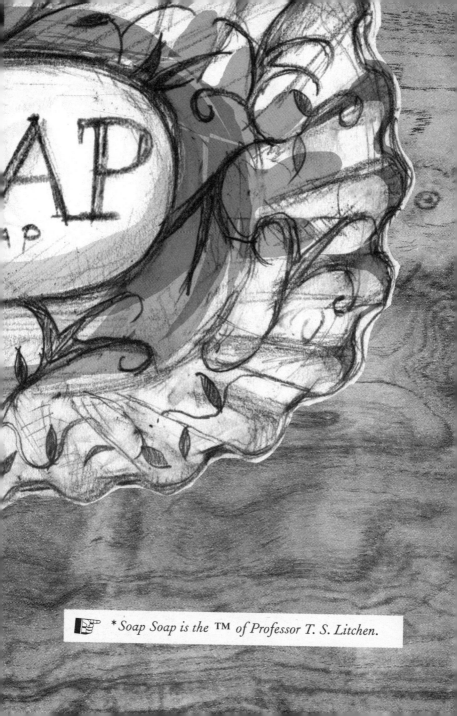

☞ *Soap Soap is the ™ of Professor T. S. Litchen.

The Bobton-Trent Dwellings

THE
B BT N-
TRENT
HOUSE
S W E E P I N G
A C R E S

AS SHOULD BE BEST-QUALITY-CRYSTAL-CLEAR
by now, the Bobton-Trents had a lot of houses,
but for the sake of simplicity these stories are
all set in the Bobton-Trents' favourite home,
Sweeping Acres.

This was a house with seven staircases and many more turrets. It was spread over a great many floors, and rambled with hallways and passages. There was a basement full of wine and old bicycles and other bits of clobber. There was an attic full of trunks and suitcases and three-legged chairs, and the usual things people seem to store and never again look at until it's time to sell up and move on. There was a grand ballroom

and a conservatory and a large salon and a small salon and a snug and a breakfast room and a dining room and a room for high tea, known as the Emerald Drawing Room,* and . . . well, etc.

Mr and Mrs Bobton-Trent's bedroom was in the east wing and had a nice view of the swan pond and the peacock avenue beyond it. The kitchen was in the Normandy extension and most of the staff rooms were up high in the south wing with

[* NAMED THE EMERALD DRAWING ROOM
not because it was emerald in colour but because the empress
of somewhere had lost an emerald earring in
a slice of gateau there.]

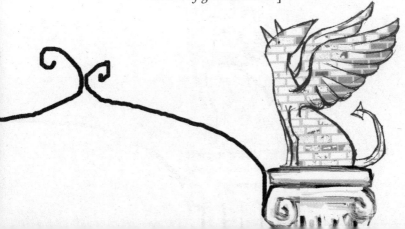

a very pleasant aspect looking on to the kitchen gardens.

Hubert's room faced mainly SOUTH and quite a bit WEST and, depending on which window he looked out from, he could see the topiary garden, the lime walk and the Winged Whippet Gates and, BEST of all, the overgrown garden next door.

Of ALL the views it was the garden
next door that *MOST* captured Hubert's
IMAGINATION,
but we'll come back
to this a bit
later on.

❧ HUBERT'S HABITAT…

Hubert Horatio's bedroom was located in the
south-west wing, up four flights of stairs towards
the far end of the floral corridor, just past the
portrait of tragic Sir Cedric Lavington, just before
the engravings of renowned deep-sea explorer
Ms Buffy Craythorne, and behind an oak-panelled
door marked: KNOCK TWICE LOUDLY
AND WAIT FOR THE WHISTLE.

It is slightly misleading to call Hubert's room a room since it was really a suite of rooms. He had his own bathroom and bedroom *of course*, and there was an adjoining room with space enough for a ping-pong table and easel, study area, climbing wall, trampoline and the usual assorted games and toys – but how many young boys can boast a laboratory? *Exactly*, not many.

On Friday evenings at approximately twenty-three minutes past six,

Mr Grimshaw (known as Grimshaw) would bring
up a silver tray bearing a lemonade fizzer (a sugary
beverage) and a chocolate-spread sandwich.
Once the sandwich had been devoured,
Hubert was ready

to play Grimshaw at table tennis, best of three.

Once the match was over, Grimshaw would then return to his formal duties, while Hubert entertained himself with some other activity before the xylophone was sounded to call everyone to supper at 8.01pm on the dot.

Grimshaw was the Bobton-Trents' butler and had been with the family a very long time and, though now getting on in years, had no intention

of retiring. Not while he could still balance a tray on his left hand and answer the telephone with his right.

Hubert had no desire for Grimshaw to retire either and did everything he possibly could to make life easier for the butler, starting with not being late for meals. Being late for meals is very annoying for the person in charge of the meals and, although Grimshaw wasn't doing the actual cooking, he *was* responsible for getting everything on the table and eaten up before it got cold. But, in any case, Hubert just didn't like to keep people waiting; as far as he was concerned it was a matter of good manners.

You could COUNT
on Hubert to . . .

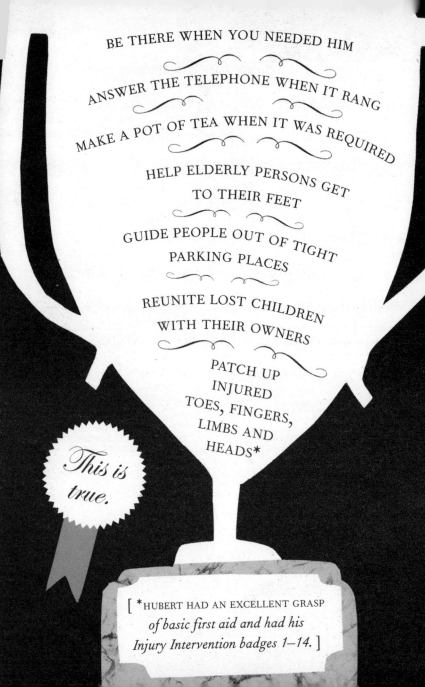

BE THERE WHEN YOU NEEDED HIM

ANSWER THE TELEPHONE WHEN IT RANG

MAKE A POT OF TEA WHEN IT WAS REQUIRED

HELP ELDERLY PERSONS GET
TO THEIR FEET

GUIDE PEOPLE OUT OF TIGHT
PARKING PLACES

REUNITE LOST CHILDREN
WITH THEIR OWNERS

PATCH UP
INJURED
TOES, FINGERS,
LIMBS AND
HEADS*

*This is
true.*

[*HUBERT HAD AN EXCELLENT GRASP
*of basic first aid and had his
Injury Intervention badges 1–14.*]

HUBERT HORATIO BARTLE BOBTON-TRENT WAS A VERY RESPONSIBLE CHILD.

Merit

II

A Respo

PERHAPS

YOU'RE ASKING YOURSELF
JUST HOW HUBERT CAME TO
BE SUCH AN EXCEPTIONALLY
RESPONSIBLE CHILD?

The answer is it really has a
great deal to do with his parents being
EXCEPTIONALLY
IRRESPONSIBLE
grown-ups.

THE DAY OF HUBERT HORATIO BARTLE'S BIRTH

December 1st was the day of Hubert Horatio Bartle's birth. Mr and Mrs Bobton-Trent had completely misremembered their baby's due date and were on holiday somewhere cold and snowy – racing huskies – when it happened. Mr Bobton-Trent, who was a terrible timekeeper, had been convinced that the child would arrive in mid-February, and Mrs Bobton-Trent was sure she was six and a half months pregnant with the world's largest baby. In fact she was exactly nine months pregnant when Hubert, who never liked to keep anyone waiting, decided it was time to be born.

☛ ASIDE

The first face he laid eyes on belonged to a husky, which is why Hubert felt strangely attached to the breed.

When Hubert was three he fell into the family's kidney-shaped swimming pool. His parents, who were playing a furious game of dominoes with the Davenport-Martins, were *utterly unaware* of their small son's plight. It was very apparent to Hubert that he would surely drown if he didn't rescue *himself*. This he did by quickly learning to swim.

Then there was the day Mrs Bobton-Trent was driving into town with the radio tuned to **High Drama FM.** So immersed was she in her radio play that she deposited Hubert at the pet parlour to have his nails clipped . . .

and dropped **Wigmore*** at the barber's,

where he found himself booked in for

A SHORT

BACK

AND

SIDES.

[**WIGMORE, the
Bobton-Trents' dog*]

And not to forget the time when Mr Bobton-Trent failed to identify the correct recreation centre and Hubert found himself on an advanced scuba-diving course rather than his scheduled activity, water-play for beginners.

Then of course there was the incident with the runaway pram . . .

but
that's
another
story.

III

The Plot

of

Land

NEVER A DULL DAY

I THINK IT'S IMPORTANT TO MENTION THAT among the many things Hubert was good at, something he had *no* trouble doing, was finding things to do. These are but a few of those things:

[I KNOW I PREVIOUSLY SAID THAT LISTS
tend to be boring, but there we go.]

Calligraphy

China restoration
Conjuring
Fossil-collecting
Wood-carving
Tree-climbing
Trampolining
Scuba diving
Flamenco dancing
Finding things
Jigsaw-puzzling
Mosaic-ing
Meditating
Knitting
Karate
Piano-tuning
Horse-whispering
Sushi-slicing
Staring out of the window
Staring into space

and
Dog training.

Hubert was positively, absolutely *never* bored and, if he was, he invented something. Very often he took up a new interest. Something Hubert had recently taken up was botany.*

And there was a great deal of botany to be had next door.

BOTANY:
the science of plant life

BOTANIST:
one who studies plants,
including fungi and algae

[* THIS INTEREST PROBABLY CAME FROM
his grandmother, who had discovered that
rarest of toadstools, the polka-dot ghost.]

The Polka-dot Ghost

Should the fungus be consumed, the eater will become deathly pale for a period of no less than seventy-eight hours, after which time they will feel fatigued and desire nothing more than to lie prone and unmoving on a cold marble floor.

The Bobton-Trent house stood next to a vacant plot . . . well, not quite vacant. It still had a small and slightly leaning-to-the-left potting shed standing in the long grass at the far end of what had once been a garden. In the garden there had

once been a house — a very beautiful and peculiar building with twisting balconies and a weathervane shaped like a dragon. The building had stood empty and neglected for so many years that finally the windows had shattered and the doors had parted from their hinges and the chimney pots had given up and fallen down and the dragon had become stuck forlornly pointing north.

The owner, Mrs Van Hibbert, had taken herself off to a care home for the fragile and infirm, and the house had been put up for sale. However, nobody seemed to want to buy the old place and no one quite knew why, though it might have had something to do with the birds.

Mrs Van Hibbert had spent her years breeding birds – the colourful singing kind. She was fond of the noise. In the very last years of her life she had liberated them, opening the doors of their ornate cages so they might roam the skies and fly to far and distant lands.

This is not what happened. All the birds had chosen to stay close to home, most of them roosting on the house or *in* the house, perched on furniture and mantelpieces. And perhaps it was this that was the problem – most people do not want to share their dwelling with several hundred birds. The dawn chorus might also have been a factor for it was very, very loud, drowning out all other sounds. Until, that is, one Monday morning

at precisely 4.42am when Mrs Bobton-
Trent was woken by an *alarming* and
thunderous crashing sound.

Maybe one too many parakeets had
decided to land on the roof that day. Maybe
the house could no longer take the strain because,
just like that, it flattened itself.

The faded "FOR SALE" sign still
stood in front of the twisted iron
gates and from time to time Hubert

90

would check his Spanish china piggy bank to see if he might perhaps have saved enough pocket money to buy the plot of land, but he was nearly always several tens of thousands short. He didn't want to ask his parents for an advance on his allowance in case something else caught his eye, like the eagerly anticipated alien exterminator splodge-gun soon to be stocked in Billings & Grimptons department store.

But, never mind, he didn't need to OWN the garden to enjoy it. Just so long as no one else bought the land he would be perfectly content.

Every day he would step out of his fifth-storey window, grab hold of the zip wire he had rigged up and sail down to the next-door wasteland. Here he would spend hours working on his treehouse and waging war on Elliot Snidgecombe. Elliot Snidgecombe was a mortal enemy and a very irritating boy with tidy hair and crease-free shorts. The very worst thing about Elliot Snidgecombe aside from his crease-free shorts was that he refused to stick to his own territory.

Instead he would regularly invade the lost garden and attempt to sneak into Hubert's treehouse and steal his stash of lemon sherbets. Worse than that, the wretch had threatened to chop down the brambles and create a croquet lawn. This could not be tolerated.

Hubert had set up various traps and tripwires, but it was a constant battle and he had to remain vigilant at all times. Mostly the two boys would hurl stale currant buns at each other and, on Thursdays, muffins.

Enjoyable though this activity was, Hubert always made sure he was back in the Emerald Drawing Room by the time Grimshaw sounded the xylophone for high tea. No matter how much he relished bombarding his enemies with currant buns, teatime was always respected.

Teatime was the Bobton-Trents' favourite hour. It was a moment to catch up on the events of the day and eat cake.*

[* VERY OFTEN HUBERT'S OWN CREATIONS,
*which his mother and father sampled with great
delight even though they were usually rather
heavy and lumpy in texture.*]

All kinds of matters were discussed.

"What could be better than cake and chatter with those you most adore?" was something Mr Bobton-Trent was very fond of saying. And when the family gathered from far and wide a long chat was chattered and a lot of cake was eaten. But gathering was easier said than done . . .

IV

Familiar

Life
Forms

E-X-T-E-N-D-E-D F-A-M-i-L-Y

LIFE FORMS

FAMILIAR

ALTHOUGH THE BOBTON-TRENTS WERE ONLY three in total, and four if you counted Wigmore the dog, which most people didn't, there were many Bobton-Trent relatives. Grandparents, great-grandparents, great-great-grandparents, aunts, uncles, great-aunts and uncles, cousins, distant cousins and cousins several times removed.

99

Hubert was endeavouring to construct a family tree for a school project he was working on, but, whenever he thought he had finished, another Bobton-Trent came to light and he was now beginning to run out of branches.

The cousins seemed to be numerous and the cousins once removed more so, and at Christmas time Hubert had trouble remembering who he had sent a card to and who he hadn't – the thing was, so *many* of his relatives had the same names.

Hubert's mother on the other hand was a Felt from the little-known Felt family who had very much dwindled in number – their heyday being some two thousand years ago.

[IF YOU HAVE EVER WONDERED *what the difference is between a second cousin and a cousin once removed (as I myself have often wondered)*, *then here's your chance to find out . . .*]

COUSINS ONCE REMOVED: Your *second* cousin is the CHILD of the *first* cousin of either one of YOUR PARENTS, whereas your *first* cousin once removed is either the CHILD of your *first* cousin or the PARENT of your *second* cousin.

☞ *Great-great-great . . . great-great . . . etc. great-great-grandma Ug Felt and her daughter, Great-great-great . . . great-great . . . great-grandma Oi Felt*

LARAMINTA-HEPSIBAR FELT
*(now Bobton-Trent), known to the
Felt family as La*

WILLARDSON-
MERRYWEATHER FELT,
*brother of La Bobton-Trent,
known as Bil (one "l")*

CONSTANTINOPLE FELT,
*who absolutely everyone knew as Con,
son of Bil and Flo, brother of Dot*

FLORA FELT *(previously Avalone)*,
married to Bil (and, once married,
had always been referred to as Flo)

EDWINA-AGNETHA FELT
(or Ed to all the family),
daughter of Cin and cousin to
La and Bil

AUNT
CINCINNATI
FELT, *who had*
never gone by any
name but Cin

DOROTHEA-
FAYBELLINE FELT,
who answered to Dot

Now there were just the six Felts, if you counted Flora Felt, formerly an Avalone, and seven of course if you remembered to include Hubert's mother. Eight if you counted Perregrine-Yapper Felt, which most people did not because she was a French bulldog dog.

☞ *Perregrine-Yapper Felt, French bulldog belonging to Flo Felt and answering to the command name, Grin.*

The Felts were a very close family (despite the fact that they were very opinionated and regularly fell out with each other) and made up for their small number by talking very loudly about themselves.

[YOU MAY KNOW SOME PEOPLE CALLED FELT
*yourself but the Felts you know are certainly
likely to be from an entirely different bloodline/
gene pool to the Cincinnati Felts.*]

No one knew why it was a tradition of the Felt family to go to all the trouble of choosing such very long and hard-to-spell names only to ruthlessly shorten them to a bare syllable, but that was the way it had always been.

Most of the Felts had relocated to Square Plains, a town built on a strict grid system with excellent signposting, the hope being that because the roads were all in straight lines it would be much easier not to get lost. This proved in the main to be true, but the problems really began when the family ventured further afield.

The Felt family were legendary for their poor sense of direction. Also their total inability to read maps, follow instructions, hold on to instructions, write down addresses in sensible places and generally keep track of useful and sometimes life-saving information. This was one of the reasons for their dwindling numbers. Mrs Bobton-Trent, being a Felt and therefore afflicted with this same

condition, was lucky enough to have a butler, a driver, a very clever son and also an intelligent dog who had a particular talent for knowing the way home. The Felts' dog Grin was useless in this regard; she had no sniffing ability and, though a charming hound, was incapable of getting from **A** to **B** sensibly. Fortunately Flo Felt was extremely organised and had an excellent sense of direction. So long as she was there things mainly went to plan.

[It is important to mention that
THE FELTS *very RARELY travelled*,
for reasons that are about to be illustrated
in the following story.]

V

The Ho

and

wling

Muttering

Noise

EXPECTING GUESTS

THE BOBTON-TRENTS WERE EXPECTING GUESTS.

They had been expecting guests for the past five

days but so far the expected guests had not

turned up.

☞ *At half past five on Tuesday afternoon,*
the Bobton-Trents stood on the steps of
Sweeping Acres, ready to greet.

By eight o'clock that same evening

they gave it up as a lost cause

*but kept
the porch
light lit*

*and
slipped
the door
key under
the mat.*

☞ *Every day thereafter they prepared breakfast, lunch and
dinner for their absent visitors in the hope that they might appear.*

"They're lost!" said La Bobton-Trent.

"I know it – they're sure to be lost!"

The expected guests were Mrs Bobton-Trent's

aunt Cin, her brother Bil and his son Con and

daughter Dot. Flo Felt was speaking at a very

116

important conference on "The Need for Multi-sensory Signposting" so was unfortunately unable to act as navigator on this occasion, and it seemed that without her guidance the journey from Square Plains to Sweeping Acres had *not* been a straightforward one.

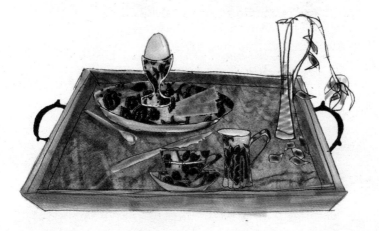

☛ *By Friday, three entire days later,*
the Bobton-Trents were rather cast down.

117

The Felts had set off late for Sweeping Acres because they had been waiting for Cousin Ed to arrive, since the plan was for her to dog-sit Grin while they were away. Cousin Ed was sorry to miss out on the trip but had decided it was unwise to visit Sweeping Acres in high summer as she was allergic to the sun. The Bobton-Trents loved the sun and were committed swimmers and poolside loungers and Ed, her skin so pale one could almost believe it to be translucent, *never* sat poolside unless it was a very dull day, preferably raining.

Grin was a recent pet acquisition, rather timid and seemingly born without even one brave bone in her small body. She was not so much a guard dog as the sort of dog to hide under a blanket at the slightest whiff of trouble. Not that Grin could sniff so much as a fly; she had no nose for *anything*, having arrived in the world without a sense of smell or direction. The thing she seemed to most enjoy was chewing things, mainly newspapers and letters. For these reasons the Felts had thought it best to leave Grin behind in the capable hands of Cousin Ed – but things had not gone according to plan.

First of all, Ed had arrived twenty-four hours early and not on the Tuesday as agreed.

Second of all, she had totally misunderstood that she was required to *stay* in the Felts' house *with* Grin. Instead she had arrived on Monday in the dead of night (so as to avoid the sun) and had carried the sleeping Grin from her kennel and into the waiting taxi, and off they had driven back to Ed's house in Fog View.

Unsurprisingly this had caused great consternation. The Felts had woken up to find Grin gone and had naturally assumed she'd been dognapped, as anyone might. Phone calls had been made, the misunderstanding explained and a new, unlikely-to-go-wrong plan was formed.

Now Cousin Ed was on her way *back* to Square Plains, *with* their dog, to dog-sit in situ while the Felts holidayed for ten days with the Bobton-Trents in glorious sunshine.

It all seemed so simple.

However, when it came to the Felts getting from

A...

to **B...**

NOTHING WAS SIMPLE.

For a start, Cousin Ed had unwisely decided to drive herself. Cousin Ed did *not* arrive in time for the handover of the door key.

The travellers delayed their journey by fourteen hours and three minutes but in the end had to make the decision to set off regardless. They hid the door key where Cousin Ed *and indeed anyone else* might be sure to find it – under the mat. They also left a note taped to the front door indicating where it had been hidden – just to be sure.

Unfortunately they were unable to telephone the Bobton-Trents to warn of their late departure because Bil had mislaid his address book and could not recall the phone number for Sweeping Acres.

The Bobton-Trent family had decided to pass the time usefully while they waited in for the Felts' knock (it is only good manners to wait in when one is expecting guests, however late they may be) and were practising for the national tiddlywinks tournament that was scheduled for September.

Second Cousin Barbara Bobton-Trent had come to stay and was helping La and Franklin improve their game and giving them a few pointers (having once been the championship title-holder).

Mr Collingsworth, a neighbour, had popped in because his stove was on the blink and he couldn't face eating another salad.

The evening was going as well as could be expected, considering Mr Collingsworth was a terrible tiddlywinks player and a poor sport. He was the sort of person who was delightful company until he took part in anything competitive.

He was about to execute a far-from-perfect flip of his tiddlywink when he stopped quite suddenly and whispered, "What was that?"

"What was what?" asked Mr Bobton-Trent, suspecting it was just another Collingsworth ploy to distract his opponents.

"That!" replied Mr Collingsworth.

Mr Bobton-Trent paused to listen. And then *he* heard it too.

"Sounded like somebody howling," he said.

"Yes," agreed Second Cousin Barbara, "it could be howling or maybe muttering."

They tried to continue with their game but found it difficult to concentrate because the howling or muttering sound was getting stronger.

"Let's call Hubert," said Mrs Bobton-Trent, reaching for the telephone. "He'll know what it is."

She dialled the south-west wing extension but there was no reply.

"He's not in his room," she announced.

128

They called down to the kitchen and the billiard room, the greenhouse and the library but no one picked up the phone.

"Of course!" said Mrs Bobton-Trent. "He will be at chess club; chess club is Wednesday night and it is Wednesday night, don't you think?"

"I thought it was Thursday," said Mr Bobton-Trent.

"Ah well, if it's Thursday then he will be at geometry club," said Mrs Bobton-Trent, flipping her tiddlywink into the high-score pot.

"What if it's Tuesday?" asked Mr Bobton-Trent.

Mrs Bobton-Trent was saved from answering this question by the arrival of Hubert himself.

i.

The Howling and Muttering Noise Continues . . .

HUBERT'S RETURN

"GOOD EVENING, MOTHER AND FATHER.

Good evening, Second Cousin Barbara.

Good evening, Mr Collingsworth."

Hubert was holding an

arrangement of two awkwardly

intertwined long-stemmed twigs

poking out of a painfully thin vase.

His parents stared at it without

understanding.

"I have been at my *ikebana*

class," explained Hubert.

"FRIDAY!" said Mr and Mrs

Bobton-Trent in unison.

132

Hubert had been studying the art of Japanese flower-arranging for some months but he was making little to no progress.

"How *lovely*," said his mother uncertainly.

"My *goodness*," said his father, stepping back two paces as if looking at a rare masterpiece.

"What on earth is THAT?" said Mr Collingsworth rather rudely.

Barbara hastily changed the subject.

"There's a noise," she said.

"What sort of noise?" asked Hubert.

"A distracting one," said Mr Collingsworth, glancing at his collection of tiddlywinks

STREWN

across

the

carpet.

133

"A terrible howling or muttering sound coming from the north wing," explained his father. "Might you know what it is?"

"It is very off-putting," said Mr Collingsworth.

Hubert listened for five minutes but could hear neither howling nor muttering.

"Perhaps it was the wind, my dear," said Mrs Bobton-Trent.

"Maybe," said Mr Bobton-Trent.

The family decided to retire for the night and as Hubert climbed the stairs of the south-west wing he considered what a very still night it was. Any howling or for that matter muttering could not have been conjured by the wind.

Hubert stayed up reading

for a couple of hours prior to

clambering into bed.

A WEEK-BY-WEEK GUIDE IN SIX HUNDRED AND EIGHTY-FIVE ISSUES*

IKEBANA

IMPROVE YOUR IKEBANA IN 685 EASY STEPS

[*Issue #1]

Before he settled in to sleep he listened out for any uncertain noises but still there was no howling or muttering that *he* could detect.

Everything seemed to be back to normal the following morning and there was no more talk of strange noises.

Though Hubert couldn't help wondering what all the little pieces of chewed paper were doing strewn up and down the corridors of the north and east wing.

As he left the house he heard his father talking on the telephone to the dog trainer . . .

136

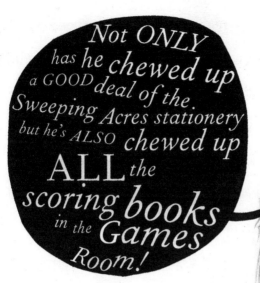

Not ONLY has he chewed up a GOOD deal of the Sweeping Acres stationery but he's ALSO chewed up ALL the scoring books in the Games Room!

This sentence struck Hubert as strange since the Bobton-Trent hound by nature was not a chewer. Clearly Wigmore was very out of sorts.

Hubert returned home at 4.30pm to find his parents sitting anxiously on the edge of their seats.

"We think it's a ghost," said his parents, rather gravely.

"*What* is a GHOST?" said Hubert.

His mother looked puzzled. "Why, a spirit of *one who is dead*, my dear child."

[SURELY HUBERT, *of all people, knew what a ghost was?*]

"I *mean,* you think *WHAT* is a ghost?" said Hubert.

"The noise!" said his mother. "At first we thought it was a *dog* ghost . . . and then we heard it *muttering*."

"Yes," said his father, "we think it's unlikely that it's a **talking** *dog* ghost so now we think it is a **talking** *ghost* who OWNS a *dog*."

"The *dog* may **also** be a *ghost* – we can't be certain," said his mother.

"But what we may be sure of is that the ghost is the reason for Wigmore's strange behaviour," said Franklin Bobton-Trent.

"Poor Wigmore," said La Bobton-Trent. "He hasn't chewed paper since he was a puppy."

"The ghost is spooking him," said Mr Bobton-Trent. Hubert always liked to be polite and he certainly would never be unkind but he was not sure he actually believed in ghosts. He went to consult his large science encyclopaedia and discovered that the science people were not big believers in ghosts either.

That night Hubert slept soundly,

and despite leaving his bedroom door ajar

heard not

even

a

p e e p

from
the
"ghost"

– or
its
dog.

ii.

The Ghost
and His Dog

AT BREAKFAST, HUBERT HORATIO COULD NOT HELP NOTICING THAT HIS PARENTS LOOKED A LITTLE TIRED.

His mother was unusually poorly groomed and his father's moustache was not in the least bit twirly. However, it must be said that the breakfast table being some eight metres long sometimes made seeing facial detail very difficult, but with the aid of a pair of opera glasses Hubert discovered all was not well with the Bobton-Trent seniors.

"We hardly slept a wink," complained his exhausted-looking father.

"Too much howling and lots of muttering," said his mother.

"And a considerable amount of chewing," added his father, pointing at the many fragments of paper that covered the carpet.

"We are going to
have to send Wigmore to
dog camp," said his mother,
looking at the mess. "Poor
Martha will be vacuuming
all day long."

At that moment Second
Cousin Barbara came staggering
into the dining room, her hand
to her brow.

"I saw it!"

she announced.

"The ghost?" asked the Bobton-Trents.

"Its dog," said Barbara. "Only it isn't a dog – it's a pig."

"A *ghost* pig?" asked La.

"An *actual* pig," replied Barbara. "A piglet, I think, although it might be a very small warthog. It moved with such $SPEED$ it was hard to tell."

"Something needs to be done," said Hubert's mother. "A ghost is one thing but a piglet on the loose is quite another."

And Hubert could only agree.

Hubert proposed that the family stay up that night and keep watch to see if they could spot the ghost and its pig in action.

He issued everyone with a rucksack containing:

① a pair of night-vision goggles

② a flask of cocoa

③ a whistle

④ a map of the house marking the zone each watcher was required to stake out

⑤ a comfortable cushion to sit on

Hubert took the far turret and adjoining attics as he was sure a ghost was more likely to haunt an attic with a turret.

It was hard to stay awake up there because it was hot, and the gurgling of the water pipes was very restful, and had it not been for the chatter of the birds in the wasteland next door Hubert would certainly have nodded off. It was a lonely business and he wished Wigmore were by his side and not at canine retraining camp.

It was almost five o'clock in the morning when Hubert heard the whistle.

He ran down the turret steps at great speed and followed the whistling sound until he reached the kitchen, where he found everyone gathered in their pyjamas, except for Zelda, the cook, who was an early riser and already had her apron on.

As it turned out, no one had actually seen the

ghost but there was some alarming evidence of its activity.

"There's been some nibbling," said Zelda.

"Nibbling?" said Mr Bobton-Trent.

"Nibbling," confirmed Zelda.

"Gracious!" said Mrs Bobton-Trent, unsure if this news was really very worrying.

"Something has helped itself to the tinned ham," said Zelda.

"Could it be a mouse?" asked Barbara.

"It used a tin-opener," said Zelda.

"It was the emergency ham," explained Grimshaw, "from the north-wing larder."

"The emergency ham?" said Mr Bobton-Trent, rising from the table dramatically.

The emergency ham was tinned and there for emergencies only, and to Franklin Bobton-Trent's mind an emergency was only really an emergency if it was a blizzard, a flood, a hurricane or a shipwreck.

He peered out of the window, and saw not even a hint of a blizzard.

☛ *An example of a tin of unopened ham, showing the special key attached to the top of the tin. This begged the question: why did the ghost use a tin-opener in the first place?*

Mr Bobton-Trent shook his head. "A ghost who can use a tin-opener is a very troubling spectre indeed."

Hubert had enormous respect for his father but really . . . was it likely that a ghost would take the trouble of wrestling with a tin-opener when it was surely capable of sticking its ghostly hands right inside the tin?

Well, maybe . . . Who could know the answer to that? But Hubert was quite certain ghosts did not eat ham, emergency or no emergency.

As Hubert climbed the seventh staircase of the east-wing shortcut he pondered this problem and only stopped pondering it when he discovered yet another trail of tiny pieces of chewed paper. He began picking them up to save Martha the chore of getting the vacuum cleaner out again, and that's when it dawned on him. Wigmore was at canine camp so couldn't possibly be responsible for this latest chew-up, so *who* was doing the chewing? And exactly where were they getting all the notepaper from?

He collected up the fragments and took them back to his room.

On some of the scraps were written words, and Hubert spent several hours trying to piece them together to form a message. But whichever way he arranged them, none of it really made much sense.

[YOU'LL HAVE TO TURN OVER
to see what I'm talking about . . .]

my room

a long

has been

Please

it

and

soon

running

for

the way

ne

The dog

me

out come show

ham is to

will cold

the

iii.

Could it Be
Ada Dupré?

JUST BEFORE BREAKFAST

THE FOLLOWING MORNING, JUST BEFORE breakfast, the Bobton-Trents were having a conference call. The Bobton-Trents frequently communicated via the internal telephone system. Sweeping Acres was such a large house it meant this was often the quickest and most practical way to have a satisfactory conversation.

"I think it's Ada Dupré," announced Barbara. She was by now well into her morning exercise regime and her voice was a little strangled from the headstand she was in.

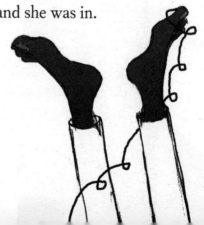

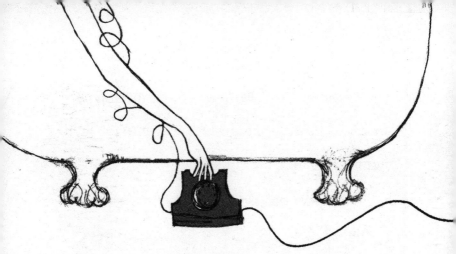

"The ghost?" asked Mrs Bobton-Trent from her bubble bath.

"I'm afraid so," said Barbara. "I saw her, and saw through her."

"But why haunt the paisley corridor?" said Mr Bobton-Trent, who was struggling into a new pair of trousers. "She always despised the north-wing extension."

"Exactly," said Barbara. "She's making her feelings known by muttering away into the small hours and eating the emergency ham."

"And who was she muttering to?" asked Mrs Bobton-Trent.

"Her dog," explained Barbara.

"But Ada never had a dog," replied Mr Bobton-Trent.

"I thought you said the dog was a pig?" said Mrs Bobton-Trent.

"I was mistaken," said Barbara. "It can't have been a pig because I distinctly heard her say, 'Where are you, you hopeless mutt?'"

"Ada Dupré always *was* very short-tempered," remarked Mrs Bobton-Trent.

"I hope she didn't catch you spying on her," said Mr Bobton-Trent.

"No, it was dark and I was hiding," said Barbara. "I thought if she saw me she might try to make me practise my scales."

Laaaaaa
Laa aa a

Ada Dupré had been a famous singing teacher and had, when she was alive, been extremely *strict* about people practising their scales. Barbara thought that Ada was the type of person who would be just as strict now she was dead, and Barbara hated singing.

Hubert was not contributing to this conversation because he was still busy trying to make sense of the words on the little chewed pieces of paper.

WHAT DID IT ALL MEAN?

The dog that was NOT a pig but *looked* like a pig.

The ghost who *might* be a short-tempered singing teacher with a taste for tinned HAM.

But *why* had she decided to HAUNT Sweeping Acres *now*?

And what was she doing *chewing up* stationery?

a long time

come

cold

Please

out

soon

is

running

the way

ham

my room

will

has been

it

the

me

The dog

and

to

show

for

At ten past ELEVEN he went down to

the elevenses room to get himself a CHELSEA BUN.

There he found Second Cousin Barbara

sipping Ceylon tea from a teacup

balanced

on her

knee.

She was looking very

S H A K E N,

rather like someone who has

just seen

a

GHOST.

iv.

The Return
of Wigmore

IT'S NOT Ada DUPRÉ

"I'VE JUST SEEN A GHOST," SAID COUSIN Barbara, "and it's not Ada Dupré, it's Cousin Ed."

"But Cousin Ed isn't dead," said Hubert.

"No," said La Bobton-Trent, walking into the room, "she's very much alive and dog-sitting Grin Felt in Square Plains."

"Well, that's a relief," said Barbara. "I've always been very fond of your cousin Ed. I would hate her to be dead."

"Me too," agreed La. "And who on earth would take care of Grin? That dog is too much for a ghost to manage."

The conversation had taken a strange turn but for Hubert things were beginning to add up . . . He just wasn't sure what *to* . . .

At half past six that evening Hubert left his room and went downstairs to see what everyone else was doing.

He found them in the Yellow Lounge furiously playing Yahtzee. Things were not going well – all the scoring pads had been chewed up and no one could find even one sheet of paper to keep track of all the points.

"I keep losing track," said Mrs Bobton-Trent. "Are you winning, Franklin, or is Barbara?"

"I think I'm winning," said Mr Collingsworth.

Mrs Bobton-Trent gave him an uneasy look.

"If only we had a slip of paper," said Mr Bobton-Trent. "Even the back of an envelope would do."

Just then Wigmore ambled in with an
envelope in his mouth.

"Wigmore, dear boy, you're back from canine
camp!" said Mr Bobton-Trent, patting the dog.

"What's that?" asked Hubert's mother.

"Looks like an envelope," said his father.

"Just what we need!" said Barbara, reaching
for it. "We can tot up the points on the back of it."

It was Hubert who did the sensible thing.
Realising that Wigmore, being an intelligent
hound, was trying to tell them something,
he took the envelope from the dog,
opened it and inside found a
letter penned in the most
beautiful handwriting.

Curiously,

it was written

on the north-wing

guest stationery.

Please somebody help me!

I think it is possible that I am in entirely the wrong house because nothing about this residence resembles the home my cousin Bil lives in – for one thing, it has stairs. I have been searching for many days to find other familiar life forms or, failing that, a way out, and have only survived thus far by eating emergency tinned ham. As a consequence I am rather dehydrated. I have written numerous messages asking for assistance and these I have left along the interminable maze of passages and stairways in the dwindling hope that someone might read them and come to my rescue. Though I wouldn't be a bit surprised if the ridiculously stupid dog I am charged with looking after has eaten them – it chews everything and the howling is driving me quite mad but this is a side issue.

This final cry for help I am throwing out of the window, my heart brimming with optimism that an intelligent creature will find it.

It is my last piece of stationery.

Yours truly,

Ed Felt

PS I am in a boldly wallpapered room, with a queen-size canopy bed, turquoise lamps and a troubling portrait of a woman called Ada Dupré. Please come soon!

Hubert did just that. He immediately deduced that the boldly wallpapered room with the Ada Dupré portrait was the Ada Dupré Grand Suite. Twenty-three minutes later he arrived back in the Yellow Lounge with Cousin Ed and Grin the French bulldog.

All was well and Ed was treated to six glasses of lemonade and a watermelon salad.

She was feeling much better by the time the front doorbell rang, and who should be shown into the house but the long-awaited Felt family.

"We got lost," said Bil Felt unnecessarily.

Following this less-than-successful visit, it was suggested by Mrs Bobton-Trent that they install a sonar system. Fortunately Hubert came up with the far better idea of weaving coloured lines into the carpets.*

[* A SIMPLE SOLUTION, *but effective. The coloured lines led visitors from their guest-room door to all the various parts of the house. A yellow line to the kitchen, red to the library, green to the garden, and so on. This system helped greatly, though it was not entirely foolproof, especially on carpet-shampooing days.*]

182

It had been three weeks since the Felts had departed and though their stay had been brief they had all very much enjoyed themselves, and there was much discussion about when they might repeat the experience, though next time with Flo Felt reading the map.

"It was fun," said La Bobton-Trent, "but I don't think I could bear to have Grin stay again. She is a terrible howler and she really got through a lot of stationery."

"Maybe I'll send Grin a voucher for canine camp," said Franklin Bobton-Trent. "After all, it did Wigmore a world of good."

Hubert gave his father a sideways look but didn't say anything. Instead he just yawned and then his mother yawned and then his father yawned. "Time to follow the indigo line," he said, getting up from his chair.

"Yes," echoed Hubert's mother, "time to take the indigo line."

"I'll fetch the cocoa," called Hubert as he made his way along the woven yellow stripe that led to the kitchen.

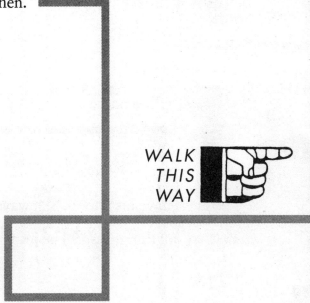

WALK
THIS
WAY

SWEEPING ACRES
CARPET MAP

NORTH WING
51.5353°N, 0.1514°W

BLACK
OBSERVATORY

D
E
N

GREEN
GARDEN

WATERMELON
BALLROOM

WEST WING
51.4464°N
0.2758°W

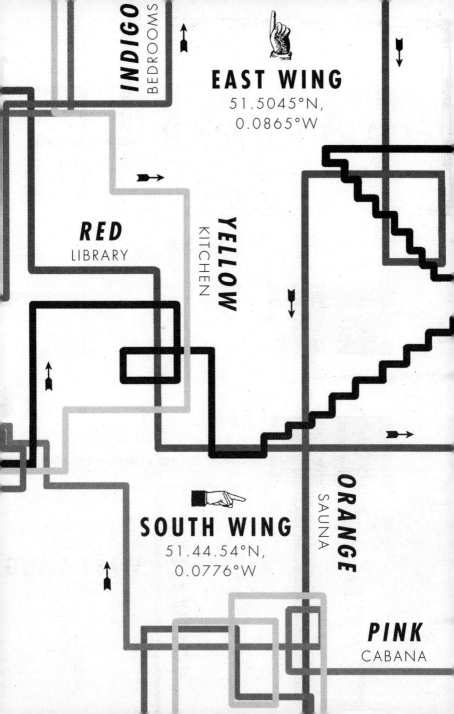

INDIGO BEDROOMS

EAST WING
51.5045°N,
0.0865°W

RED LIBRARY

YELLOW KITCHEN

SOUTH WING
51.44.54°N,
0.0776°W

ORANGE SAUNA

PINK CABANA

Hubert had been making cocoa since he was

a baby. His parents seemed incapable of preparing

the beverage themselves and, try as he might

to educate them in the art, they simply couldn't

master the method. But Hubert, who was not a

giver-upper, was determined to teach them.

After all, one day they might need to do it

all

by

themselves.

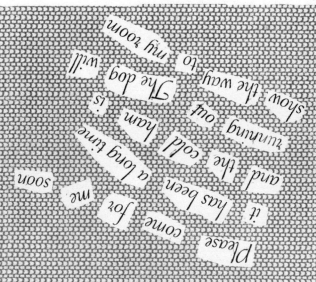

Epilogue

THE FINAL PLOT

THE NEXT MORNING, HUBERT AWOKE WITH
the lark . . . or was it the parakeet? He was in an
excellent mood because he had learned that Elliot
Snidgecombe was away visiting his grandmother,
so there would be no bun-throwing today. Hubert
had decided to devote this time to constructing a
fourth floor on his treehouse; he needed more of a
bird's-eye view of his mortal enemy's lair.

This would mean making some alterations to his pulley system. The pulley system was a contraption created mainly for the benefit of his dog, Wigmore. As a rule, dogs cannot climb trees and no amount of teaching or indeed shouting will make it so.

Hubert had learned this lesson the hard way.

His many attempts to coax Wigmore into two pairs of "grip like a cat" climbing shoes (Hubert's own invention) had been unsuccessful and had resulted in Wigmore hiding out for several hours in the potting shed. Hubert had solemnly promised not to put either of them through this unpleasant experience again.

Anyway, back to today.

Hubert felt great happiness as he zip-wired down to the wilderness next door and raced through the long grass towards his den. He didn't even feel a bit bothered when he tripped over the fallen tree and fell into some stinging nettles; nothing was going to blight this day. He looked around for a dock leaf. There was no shortage of them – they grew all over the garden – but he knew that there were some *especially* large ones growing up by the twisty iron gates.

He began winding his way towards them, stepping over brambles and pushing through the umbrella bamboo using his penknife to cut a pathway. He realised he had reached his destination when he bumped his head on the old **"FOR SALE"**

sign that stood just inside the gates.

It hurt quite a lot and his eyes went a bit blurry. He hoped he didn't have concussion. He tried to focus on something just to make sure and looked up at the estate agent's sign with its fading words and bleached-out colour. Only . . .

How strange, thought Hubert, for the letters on the sign today looked very bright and very in focus.

And there was something *else* strange about them.

No longer did the seven letters spell two words, "FOR SALE".

Now there were just *four* big letters spelling just one word . . .

Hubert blinked in disbelief – all that money he had worked so hard to save, sitting there in the Spanish china pig. He had missed his chance; his beloved plot of land was sold.

And that, as they say, is that.

Well, for now at least, since there is a further tale to tell, but you will have to go and find it in another book because this one is quite finished.

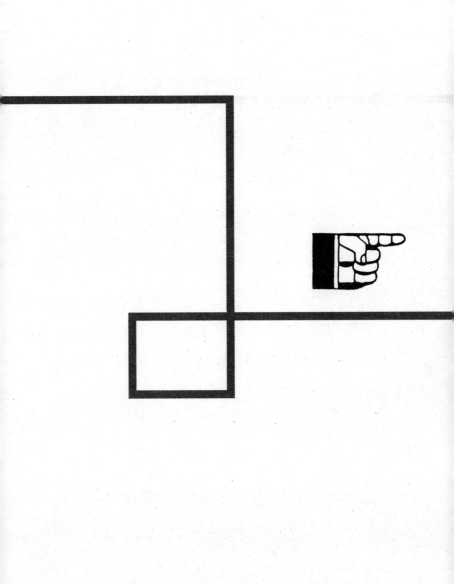

ACKNOWLEDGEMENTS

MANY YEARS AGO AN ESPECIALLY INSPIRING school friend introduced me to the deliciously disrespectful schoolboy Nigel Molesworth, famous creation of Geoffrey Willans and Ronald Searle. I could spend a long time listing what I love about the Molesworth books but one of the most appealing things for me is that as many pages are devoted to pictures as to text. It is this balance between the written and visual telling of the story that gives the character such presence and makes the books so engagingly funny. There is no obvious format for how things are set out; there are long passages with incidental illustration, pages of pictures with sharp, witty captions, typed letters and notes, character portraits and scenes. There is a story in there but there are many digressions and comic asides along the way.

It is this unconventional way of putting a book together that inspired me to write this one. Though Hubert Horatio is entirely different in terms of character, plot and voice, I do owe Willans and Searle a great debt for showing me that it is possible to create a book that is neither chapter book, picture book nor novel,

neither graphic novel nor comic strip. A book
that can be enjoyed, whether read from beginning
to end, or, should you prefer, by dipping in and
reading favourite pages. I have rarely enjoyed
creating anything as much as I have this, and
I hope it will appeal to anyone of any age.

Along with Geoffrey Willans and Ronald
Searle, I would also very much like to thank
my friend and designer David Mackintosh, who
helped me enormously when it came to bringing
the character to the page. He understood exactly
what I was trying to achieve and designed the
book exquisitely. I would also like to thank
Goldy Broad for added design elements and
for the beautifully realised cover. Thanks too

to Alice Blacker, my editor, and to Ann-Janine Murtagh, my publisher. Last of all, a very special thank you to Philippa Perry, who worked so hard to promote my very first Hubert book (many years ago, way back in 2004). It is she who encouraged me to return to the world of the Bobton-Trents and I am very grateful for that.

Lauren Child

to Alice Blacker, my editor, and to Ann-Janine Murtagh, my publisher. Last of all, a very special thank you to Philippa Perry, who worked so hard to promote my very first Hubert book (many years ago, way back in 2004). It is she who encouraged me to return to the world of the Bobton-Trents and I am very grateful for that.

Lauren Child

3.14159265358 9

50288 41971 6939 937

3164 062 862 0899 862

4 8086513282 306 64

5 35 9 408 1 2848 11
72

1 05559 644 6 2 2948 9

756 659 3 3446 128 4756

09 1 456 48566 923 4

3 39 6072 60249 141
3

381 48 15209 2 096

3 9 2 5 9 36 0011 330

146 519 4 511 6 094

30 2 186 173 8 1 932
9 21 1

52 3 79 962 749567 351

8301 1 9 491 29 83367 3